My Dog Laughs

RACHEL ISADORA

Nancy Paulsen Books

To Mocha and all her friends

Nancy Paulsen Books
an imprint of Penguin Random House LLC
Visit us at penguinrandomhouse.com

Nancy Paulsen Books is a registered trademark of Penguin Random House LLC.

Library of Congress Cataloging-in-Publication Data is available upon request.

Manufactured in China by RR Donnelley Asia Printing Solutions Ltd.
ISBN 9780399173851
Special Markets ISBN 9780593111741 Not for Resale
3 5 7 9 10 8 6 4 2

Design by Marikka Tamura.
Text set in Archer.
The art was done in ink and watercolor.

This Imagination Library edition is published by Penguin Young Readers, a division
of Penguin Random House, exclusively for Dolly Parton's Imagination Library,
a not-for-profit program designed to inspire a love of reading and learning, sponsored
in part by The Dollywood Foundation. Penguin's trade editions of this work are
available wherever books are sold.

I MEET MY DOG

I name my dog.

This is Olivia.   This is River.

And this is Paco, Munchey, Daisy, and Josie.

My dog looks like me!

Nice smile

Nice eyes

Nice graceful feet

My dog dances!

Nice posture

Nice red hair

My dogs look like each other.
They are sisters.

My dog is as big as me.

You're so big!

Mine is *so* small.

My dog and cat
are the same size.

GETTING TO KNOW MY DOG

My dog loves belly rubs.

Mine likes to
watch TV with me.

My dog likes to lick!

Mine too!

That tickles!

My dog is sad when I leave.

My dog cries!

My dog follows me everywhere . . .
even into the bathroom!

My dog farts a lot.

P.U.,
Winston!

My dog gets checkups,
just like me.

It's okay,
Charlie!

My dog likes
to cuddle.

Sometimes my dog
sleeps in my bed.

Sometimes I sleep
in his bed.

My dog likes to sleep a lot!

My dog dreams!

I TRAIN MY DOG

Here are some commands . . .

Sit!

Stay!

Lie down!

Leave it.

No jumping.

Good doggie.

My dog tries hard but sometimes
makes mistakes . . .

*Oops!
I had an accident.*

*Go here,
Pearl.*

This pee-pee pad is for you.

Uh-oh!

I'm in trouble.

These chew toys are for you.

Sometimes my dog wants my dinner . . .

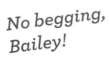
No begging, Bailey!

The food I eat can make you sick. No grapes!

This is your dinner.

Don't drink from
the toilet.

You drink from
your bowl.

And I drink from
my glass.

GOING OUT WITH MY DOG

My dog wears a collar,
a name tag, and a leash.

My dog has a red harness.

Mine has a blue leash.

Sometimes my dog
wears a coat,

a sweater,

a raincoat,

or boots.

In the car, we all wear
our seat belts.

*Let's go,
Carlos!*

I take my dog outside
when he has to pee.

*Good boy,
Rocco.*

When my dog poops, I clean up after her.

My dog loves going
to the park.

My dog has lots of friends.

My dog eats worms.

No, Spike!

Yuck!

My dog chases squirrels . . .
but never catches any.

My dog howls at fire engines.

Mine barks at skateboarders.

No, Rufus!

MY DOG PLAYS

My dog plays with her friends.

My dog plays with me.

My dog can catch anything!

Bravo,
Pokey!

My dog likes to do all
the things I do . . .

We paint.

We dance.

We dress up.

We dig.

We watch the waves.

My dog snuggles!

I LOVE MY DOG

My dog makes me feel better
when I am sick.

My dog loves me
even when I strike out.

My dog celebrates my birthday.

Happy birthday to you!

My dog sings!

My dog waits for me.

Mine helps with my homework.

My dog is always happy to see me.

Mine too!

My dog thinks I'm funny . . .

My dog laughs!